McGovern

P9-DCQ-248

Around and About

Maps and journeys

Kate Petty
and Jakki Wood

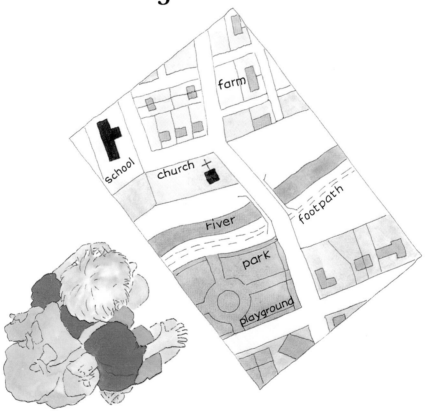

BARRON'S

First edition for the United States, Canada, and the Philippines published 1993 by Barron's Educational Series, Inc.

© Copyright by Aladdin Books Ltd 1993

Designed and produced by
Aladdin Books Ltd
28 Percy Street
London W1P 9FF

All rights reserved
No part of this book may be reproduced in any form by photostat, microfilm, xerography, or any other means, or incorporated into any information retrieval system, electronic or mechanical, without the written permission of the copyright owner.

All inquiries should be addressed to:
Barron's Educational Series, Inc.
250 Wireless Boulevard
Hauppauge, NY 11788

International Standard Book
No. 0-8120-1235-6

Library of Congress
Catalog Card No. 92-30581

Library of Congress Cataloging-in-Publication Data

Petty, Kate.
Maps and journeys / Kate Petty–1st ed.
p. cm. – (Around and about)
Includes index.
Summary: Harry measures his yard, maps the streets near his house, draws nearby landmarks, and finds out all about making and reading maps.
ISBN 0-8120-1235-6
1. Map drawing–Juvenile literature. [1.Map drawing. 2. Maps.] I. Title. II. Series: Petty, Kate. Around and about.
GA130.P396 1993
526–dc20   92-30581   CIP   AC

Printed in Belguim

3456 4208 987654321

Design David West Children's
Book Design
Illustrator Jakki Wood
Text Kate Petty
Consultants Keith Lye B.A.,
F.R.S.G.,
Eva Bass Cert. Ed., teacher of geography to 5-8 year-olds

Contents

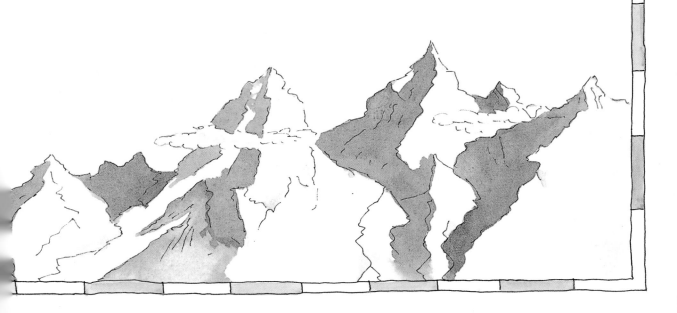

Hi..I'm Harry and this is...

..R..Ralph!

Don't get lost

Meet Harry and his dog, Ralph.
They like to travel all over the place.
Harry wants to find his way around without getting lost, so he's going to learn about maps.

Ralph, where are you?

A view from above

When Harry and Ralph walk along
the street, they can't see what's around the
corner. But when they look down from a
balloon, they can see everything laid out.
They can see the church and
the station and all the
roads in between.

A map or a plan of a place is like the view from above.

Drawing a plan

Harry and Ralph decide to make a plan of the garden. They can see its shape from above.

Harry walks from the front of the garden to the back. It is 30 steps long. Then he walks from one side to the other. It is 16 steps wide.

Harry draws his steps on the paper.
Now he wants to put in the rose
tree and the pond. How can
he find out exactly where
to put them?

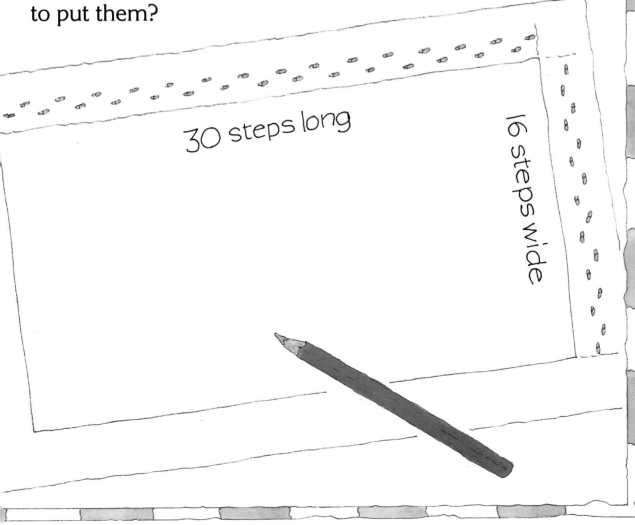

30 steps long

16 steps wide

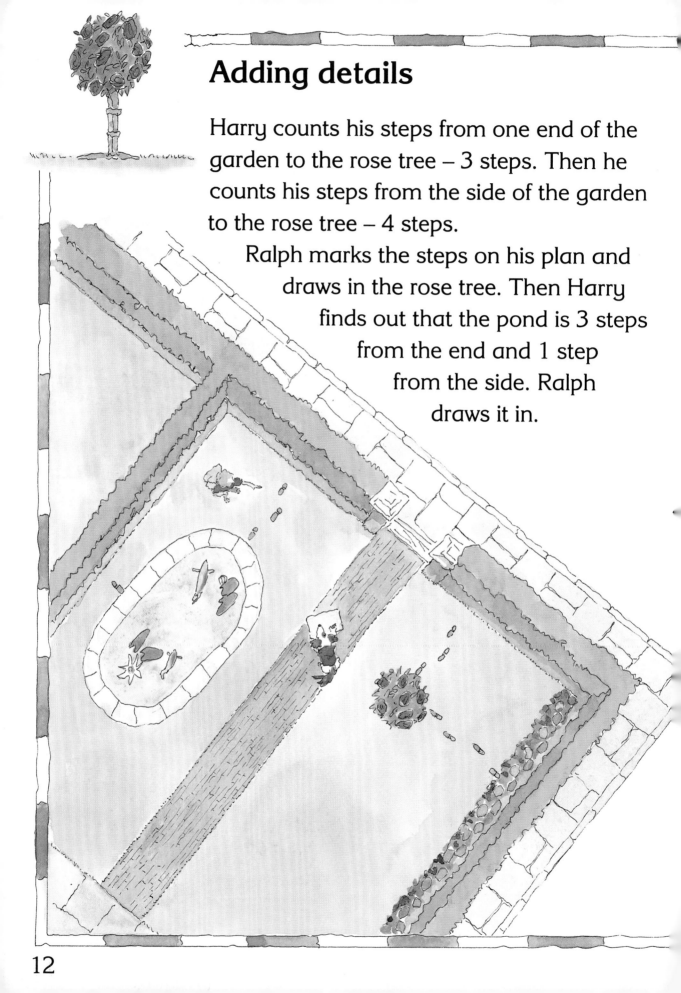

Adding details

Harry counts his steps from one end of the garden to the rose tree – 3 steps. Then he counts his steps from the side of the garden to the rose tree – 4 steps.

Ralph marks the steps on his plan and draws in the rose tree. Then Harry finds out that the pond is 3 steps from the end and 1 step from the side. Ralph draws it in.

Ralph measures the garden with a tape measure. It is 60 feet (18 meters) long, which means that one of Harry's steps is 2 feet (0.6 meter) long. They draw a scale on their plan. Make a plan of your garden or your classroom.

= 2 feet

The route to school

Look at the picture opposite. It shows Harry's school at the top, the church in the middle, and Harry's house at the bottom. Below, Harry is making a map of his way, or route, to school. He thinks hard about where he turns left and where he turns right. He draws in landmarks, which are special things like the bridge and the church that he sees on the way. He marks in his route.

Now you do the same for a
short trip that you know well.

Street plans

Here is a street plan of the roads that Harry drew. What are the differences between the two maps? Harry's map shows landmarks that are important only to him and Ralph. The street plan has different landmarks. What are they?

Compare your map with a street plan of the same area. What differences can you see?

Landmarks

There are different ways of showing a special feature on a map.

You can label it.

You can draw it.

Or you can draw a symbol, which is a special sign.

Here are some other symbols that are used on maps.

windmill   motorway   zoo

bridge   picnic   campsite

airport   wildlife park   beach

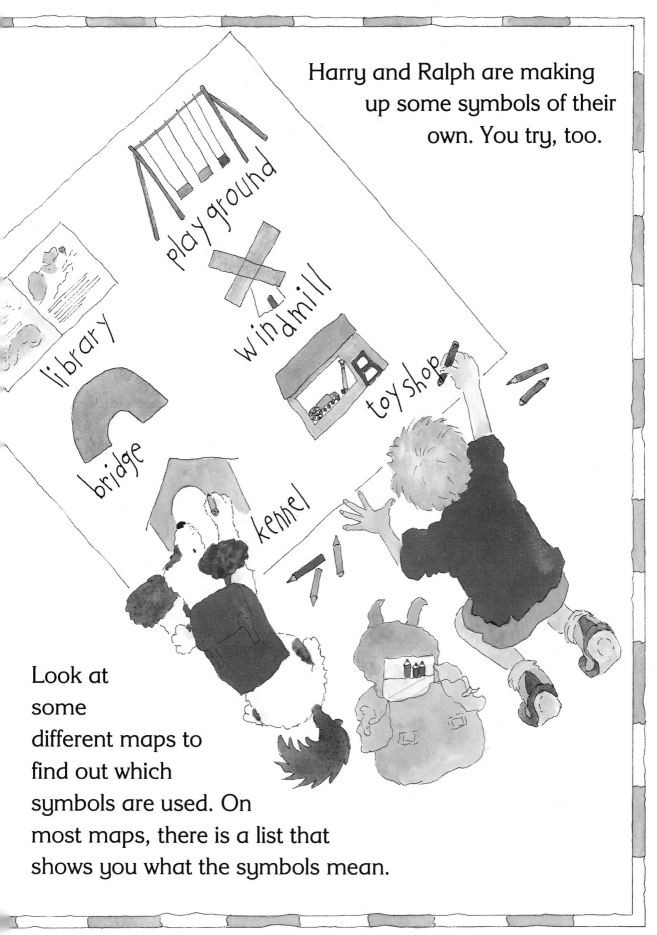

Harry and Ralph are making up some symbols of their own. You try, too.

library

playground

windmill

toyshop

bridge

kennel

Look at some different maps to find out which symbols are used. On most maps, there is a list that shows you what the symbols mean.

North, South, East, West

Harry and Ralph already understand the directions left, right, up, and down. Now they want to learn about north, south, east, and west. They look at a globe. The North Pole is at the top and the South Pole is at the bottom. Maps are usually drawn with north at the top and south at the bottom too. West is left and east is right.

A magnetic compass shows you where north is.

Which direction are you facing?

The treasure map shows:

🏴‍☠️

12 paces west
×
12 paces south
×
15 paces southeast

🏴‍☠️

Here is a map of a treasure island. It shows how the pirates found the treasure. Southeast is half way between south and east.

Making maps

Most modern maps are based on photographs taken from the air. A plane flies back and forth across the area to be mapped (just like mowing a lawn.) A camera in the floor of the plane takes photographs of the ground beneath.

When the photos are put together, like a jigsaw puzzle, the map maker has all the information needed to start drawing a map.

Using a map is simpler than making one.

That way is north.

Natural features

Every place has some feature that makes it special, and different from other places. There may be a river, or a forest, lakes, or mountains. The place may be by the ocean or in the middle of a huge expanse of land. A wide river runs through the middle of Harry's town.

Make a list of the natural features of the place where you live. How would you show them on a map?

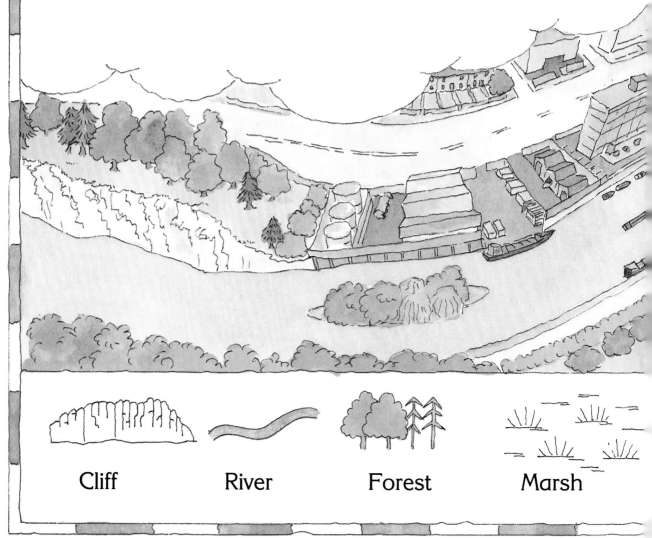

| Cliff | River | Forest | Marsh |

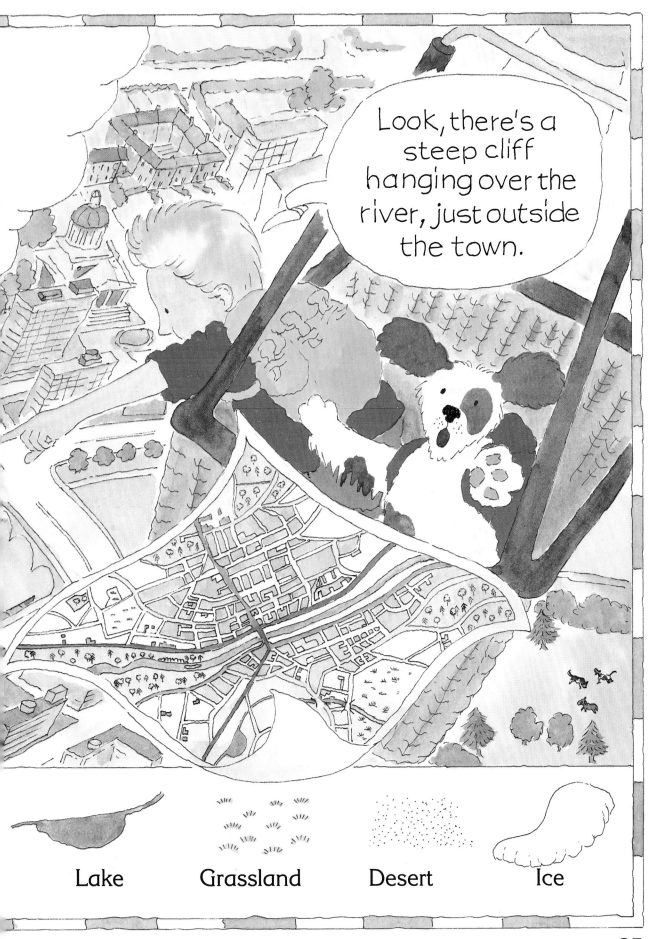

Lake   Grassland   Desert   Ice

Up and away

Harry and Ralph go up in their balloon to find out about the places beyond their town. They can see the town and the river. To the west the river leads to a big city and the ocean. Small villages are built beside it to the east, where there are woods. There are hills to the north of the river. To the south there is a highway that leads to another city, passing more towns along the way. Harry and Ralph find the landmarks on their maps.

Up and away, we're off to see the rest of the world now.

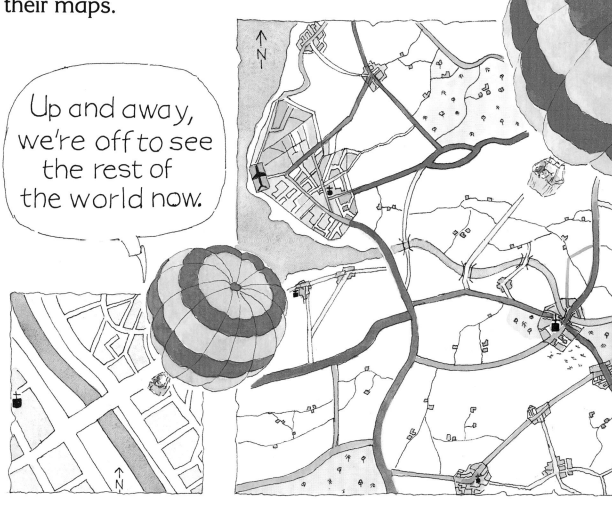

As Harry and Ralph rise higher and higher they can see more of the Earth beneath them. They need maps that show a bigger area, drawn to a smaller scale.

Looking at an atlas

Find your town in an atlas. Is it anywhere near the ocean? If you live in a small town, what is the nearest big city called? Look for the name of your state or province.

Now Harry and Ralph need never get lost!

Index

This index will help you to find some of the important words in the book.